COAST TO COAST

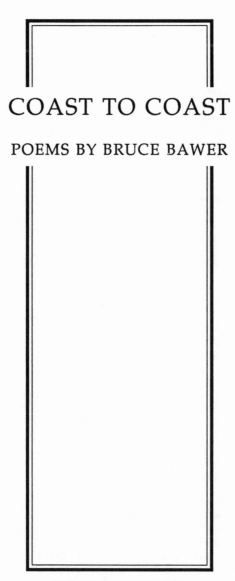

COAST TO COAST

POEMS BY BRUCE BAWER

STORY LINE PRESS

1993

This publication was made possible thanks in part to the generous support of the Nicholas Roerich Museum, the Andrew W. Mellon Foundation, the National Endowment the Arts, and our individual contributors.

ISBN: 0-934257-51-5

Book design by Lysa McDowell

Published by Story Line Press, Inc.
Three Oaks Farm in Brownsville, OR 97327

Some of the poems in this collection originally appeared in the following periodicals:
Agni: "Jeremy"
The American Scholar: "Art and Worship"
Anglican Theological Review: "Confirmation"
The Arizona Quarterly: "The View from an Airplane at Night, over California"
Boulevard: "Fur," "The Jogger," "The Snow Boy"
Chelsea: "Communion"
Crosscurrents: "California"
The Hudson Review: "A Letter to Cambridge"
The Kansas Quarterly: "Mount Hope"
The New Criterion: "Grand Central Station, 20 December 1987"
Paris Review: "Gloves," "Beginning," "August Night," "ASPCA"
Pequod: "Saxophone"
Poetry: "Beach"
Poetry East: "Thirteen"
Southwest Review: "August"
Verse: "Ferry," "Devotions"

"Malibu, January" and "On Leaving the Artists' Colony" first appeared in *Innocence*, a chapbook published by the Aralia Press.
"The View from an Airplane at Night, over California" also appeared in *The Anthology of Magazine Verse and Yearbook of American Poetry*.
I wish to extend my thanks to the Djerassi Foundation and to its former director, Sally Stillman, for a residency during which I wrote some of these poems and prepared an earlier version of this manuscript. I wish also to thank Dick Allen, Gloria Brame, Alfred Corn, Dana Gioia, Phillis Levin, Robert McPhillips, Michael Peich, Robert Phillips, and Harriet Zinnes for their interest, advice, and encouragement.

For Christopher,
"bearer of Christ"

CONTENTS

CONTENTS

II

CONTENTS

III

C O N T E N T S

III
(Continued)

I

SAXOPHONE

Walking down Seventh Avenue in the snow
I turn down Forty-eighth Street and see
a dozen guitars hanging in a window.
Lord, it's the place where I bought my saxophone.
Suddenly I remember: twelve years old,
my voice about to change, the instrument
heavy in my hands, bright gold, ice cold.
I blew my lungs out, but it only brayed.
The salesman reached out, took it away from me,
wiped the mouthpiece on his sleeve, and rent
the warm air with a perfect, bell-like tone.
My father and I smiled, and the salesman played
an old, familiar Hoagy Carmichael song,
and the stockboy put down a box and sang along.

POEMS FOR BRIAN

1. BEACH

Twelve years old and nearly as tall as I,
my cousin's stunning son draws his big toe
through the cool firm sand at Rockaway.
"This is my net," he says, his voice as low
as mine, his fingers stroking his slim thigh,
his blond hair tousled on this early May
morning, "and that one's yours." He's tireless.
We've played catch for an hour or so, I guess,
up by the boardwalk, where the chalk-white sand
burned our soles, making us hop from foot
to foot, as if stomping grapes on the strand,
and now (at his insistence: he's put
himself in charge, this tall, no-longer-shy
basketball star of the seventh grade)
we've moved down to the cooler waterside
to play soccer; he's mapping out the field
by drawing in the sand. "All right," I sigh,
unwilling, though exhausted, to forswear
this blessed sport with youth. He cocks his head,
brushes his fingers quickly through his hair,
assumes a cougar's pose, his blue eyes steeled,
his long eyelashes disconcertingly
feminine, looking for all the world
like some Athenian lad about to be

immortalized, three thousand years ago,
in marble; and then, quite suddenly,
without so much as a terse "Here we go,"
he rolls his tennis ball onto the sand,
as if he's bowling, and runs swiftly at
the thing, fleet-footed as a wiry cat.
Eyes cool, jaw set, puppet arms and hands
dangling beside his baggy, sky-blue shorts,
he kicks the ball, scores, speeds on, turns his slim
body gently—slowing, sailboat-like,
with the turn (how I marvel at him!)—
and, with a gorgeous, graceful, gull-like swoop,
sweeps up the ball, spins, and tosses it,
as if this were the school gym, I the hoop.
Clumsy, feeling hopelessly antique
(much more, at least, than twenty-eight), I catch
the ball and roll it off my palm; he crowds,
steals, I press him, slip my foot between
his own, and steal the ball back with a sleek
kick of which I feel absurdly proud.
I score the goal, but don't move fast enough:
the ball rolls into the shallow, slows, and stops.
I splash in after it; my ankles freeze,
the sea salt stings my soles. I bend down,
plunge my left hand in, wrap it around
the ball, walk back toward him and try to squeeze
the green thing dry, as if it were a lime.
"No! Don't do that," he orders. What does he mean?
What, my eyes implore, have I done this time?

"The ball," he explains. "You're standing on the field.
You're not supposed to have it in your hand."
"Oh." I feel like a dope. (How can this boy
make me feel dumb, when brilliant minds cannot?)
Tentatively, I throw the ball, the hot
sun on my back, and kick; it splatters sand
on him; we scramble for it—then all
at once we're both on top of that green ball,
flexing, blocking, kicking up huge, wet
clumps of sand onto each other's shins,
circling, glancing, as if the dance had been
choreographed for us by Fred Astaire.
Toe to toe, nose to nose, wrist to thin
wrist—close enough for me to glimpse each fine
eyelash and blue iris, to smell his sweat,
to see the sand grains scattered in his hair,
and note that his legs are as long as mine—
we madly maul the ball, our nearly bare
bodies blazing, and both move beyond
our separate lives, into another state
to which there are no words that correspond,
where our minds, for a moment, celebrate
a rare communion; he looks at me, hot
and pink and perspiration-damp, his blond
hair matted, eyes pellucid as a pond
yet pierced with a pure, perfect happiness,
the same as mine; and how we manage not
to touch at all is anybody's guess.
And suddenly the moment's passed. He gets

the ball, and shoots it straight into his "net."
And, twenty minutes later, when he's shot
the winning goal, then turned to me and grinned
gloriously (as if to tell me, *I'd
be just as glad if you'd been the one to win*),
I—muscles aching, sand-caked, my skin fried
red—grin back at him and think of all
the summers that lie before him, bright and wide
as a white, sun-swept beach; and as we fall
to our exhausted knees, the tide steals in,
erases both our nets, and steals the ball.

2. THIRTEEN

Brian is troubled. On this October day
he sits here with my aunt, his grandmother,
and quietly fidgets in a kitchen chair
while I stand staring at him from the doorway.

Last time I saw him was six months ago.
Surprising that he hasn't grown since then:
he's still shorter than I, five-ten or so,
still blond, blue-eyed, and singularly thin.

He's changed, though. Handsome now, not beautiful,
he looks less like a child, more like a teen.
A fine blond mustache sprouts above his lip
and fire-red blotches mar his milk-white skin.

One day last year I visited him at camp
and on his cabin steps, beneath the trees,
he greeted me with a sweet, ingenuous smile
and a startlingly delicate kiss upon the lips.

But now he's wild. He's run away from home
not once but twice this year; the second time
he made it more than thirty miles before
he climbed into a helpful stranger's car.

This summer the camp sent him home for stealing.
And he keeps buying cigarettes, and smoking,
and won't say where the money's coming from.
Today, when he arrived, he shook my hand.

And now he sits here, looking miserable,
shy as well as supercilious,
as if we were his teachers, or the police.
He idly slides his palm across the table,

then squirms and twitches like a drowning man.
When asked a question he screws up his face,
mumbles, shrugs, and looks down at his hands.
He isn't really in the room with us.

Almost fourteen, he's gone to seek a place
where home and family are not everything,
and loved ones do not die or get divorced:
a place where he can run free and be strong.

How can I tell him that there's no way out,
that throughout his life he'll bear the weight
of childhood sorrow, and grow used to it—
that that is what it means to be adult?

There is no way at all. His heart's language
is different from mine. To see the boy
is to remember myself at his age,
and to realize there's nothing I can say.

COMMUNION

My cat is snoring
in her Clorox box turned sideways
to face the warm radiator.

I stand at the kitchen counter
waiting for coffee water to boil
in the new aluminum pot,

and read the blue-bound proof
of a famous poet's letters.
I think of what they said tonight

on the news: that it would snow
all night, all day tomorrow.
I think of the boy with herpes,

the latest subway murder,
the new talks in Geneva.
And I remember the report

about the gorilla in Chicago
whose kitten friend was killed
by a car. They told the gorilla,

in sign language, and she cried.
The poet writes his wife: "When notes
get down below a certain pitch,

they are apprehended by the ear
not as sound, but as pain."
My cat wakes up, and yawns,

and looks at me. Outside the window,
white flakes fill the darkening sky.
I turn a page. The water sings.

FUR

My dead uncle's suits have taken possession of
my closet, and his bottles of after-shave
now crowd the bathroom shelves. It is strange
to have these things around. Opening
a bottle, I smell death; putting
on one of the suits, I feel death
wrap itself around me, squeeze my arms
and hug me by the shoulders.

I put the suit back on its hanger, and escape
the dark house for backyard sun.
My cat strolls over, purrs, rubs
against my leg, flops at my feet. I pick
her brush up from the edge of the back step
and run it through her thick brown fur,
which I pull off in a clump and toss
on the pavement. I brush the cat again.
She rolls on her back, stretches
with a shiver. Then, suddenly, something catches
her eye. She starts like a cougar,
flips into a predator's crouch. I turn
to see her prey: a sparrow swooping down to grab

for its nest that thick brown clump of
brushed-out fur, which the wind has sent
skipping down the driveway like a
tumbleweed. Amazed, I watch the bird rise,
the brown clump of fur in its beak,
and head for its home on a maple branch.

MIMOSA

I'm feeling Dickinsonian tonight—
arrayed in white, propped in a window seat,
listening to distant voices singing,
staring at the closed leaves of my tree.

Once this tall mimosa was a weed
in the backyard, among the grass and vines.
It stood shin-high. I could have pulled it out
with my left hand and tossed it in the trash.

Now its branches reach across the yard
like fingers hovering above a breast,
and, here on the upper floor, its small
pink flowers press against my window screen.

ASPCA
for Sari

That day in winter: the rows
of shabby cages, stacked
like death-camp bunkbeds,
in which tiger kittens gamboled,
young toms hissed or dozed
in corners, old tabbies stared
unblinkingly at us
as if they knew their fate,
and a chipper black-
and-orange-and-white cat
rose up to greet us—as if we were
her family, returned home
at the end of day—and nuzzled
the bars of her cage,
to which a three-by-five
card was affixed, decreeing
the date of her demise.

But you were there to issue
a reprieve, and it was
her fate you foiled: checking
her sex, you opened
the cage and carried her
into a world of privilege—

a world of kind
and deferential vets, of bright
windowsills on sunny days,
of arms that plucked
her briskly from the brink
to warm her in the night. How
easy it was, to save a life
and to bestow a home!

Yet every so often I rise
from unsettling sleep, trembling
with the memory of those
others: the ones who hissed
at us, who were too old
or young, or ill or male,
the ones who were fast
asleep when we made
our rounds, and who never knew
how close they'd come
to salvation;
and trembling especially
with the memory
of a certain tom, his fur
shimmering and black
as a sable coat, who gaped
at me, inexplicably startled,
when I entered the place
of death, whose eyes pursued me

with uncanny fascination,
as if he thought that I
were the one who held his life
in my hands, and who,
when we departed, the carrier
newly heavy in your hand,
met my gaze as if he understood.

LONG ISLAND POEMS

1. I Was Always

I was always so careful about friends,
letting them in gradually,
one step at a time;

then you came, and pushed
your way in. Inside of a month
you had struck my vitals

which you now move in
and out of so casually,
each time letting blood.

2. The Snow Boy

He came from sunny California
to Long Island,
skis and ski poles and ski togs ready
for snow. It was August.

He waited. Months went by
and it grew colder, and he grew warmer
and mostly more complicated. Every so often
he reminded you that he wanted *snow*.

He could be so exasperating sometimes;
but he leaned on you so, and so you cared—
yes, even about the snow,
which you were sure would come soon—

But winter was barren.
January passed, and February—
no snow. And he chilled
toward you, if no one noticed but yourself...

You agonized. And then in March, at last,
the snows came. And as you plodded through
    the drifts
that night, he called from behind:
"Carry me."

And he was light in your arms as you crunched
    along the path.

3. A LETTER TO CAMBRIDGE

    This is just to let you know
that every night I lie awake in bed,
    my mind feverishly full of you,
    and only fall asleep exhaustedly
    when the sky begins to lighten
outside my window, and birds sing.

So riven are we from one another
this long year, it's hard to believe
you're really there, in Cambridge,
    following some mysterious pike,
the one road of your life, while I
    bear your year-old memory down

this lonely road of mine, which
    grows stranger daily, and look up
    every so often to see the memory
growing stranger too. That's
    the most painful thing of all—
        to see memory yield to the mind's

daily perversions, and the mind
unable to desist. Have you seen it,
    how time folds fancy into memory?
I'd never noticed it before.
    Now that I have, though, I realize
that none of us dies all at once.

    From the moment that a moment
    enters the memory, it begins
to feed on fantasy and fear.
    Memory mixes with desire, never
to be divorced. The past cannot
    move into the present uncorrupted.

That is why I reach out to you now,
    not as a beloved, myth-laced memory,
   but as a friend, estranged, in Cambridge.
Please do not think me tiresome
   for troubling you with memory. I ask
    nothing of you but a moment's thought.

ON THE ROAD

It is long past midnight, and I am alone
on the highway, speeding after the moon
as it runs from the racing dawn.
Movement brings me calm. I glide
as if across a lake, whose waters
churn below, while I fly westward—
far from home, but headed there.

JEREMY

Pregnant, young, abandoned
in California
by the glamorous husband
nobody in the family ever saw,
Nita went back
to Carolina, that summer, for
her *accouchement*.

She named the baby Jeremy
and raised him in a small pine
house on Palmetto.
Determined to give him The Best,
she lived by the motto:
"Nothing's too fine
for Jeremy!" So did he.

They were a unit, two in one—
"Nita and Jeremy."
Growing up, I never heard
the names pronounced separately.
To anyone who'd listen, she'd
declare: "I don't need
a man, I have my son."

Two years my senior,
he always struck me as utterly

exotic. Apple-cheeked,
husky, a bit taller than I,
he'd gush for hours
about the Little Theatre,
horses, and antiques.

At summer's end, luxuriating
in my Dad's parked Cadillac,
he'd beg in actressy
tones: "Oh, take me back
to New York with
y'all!" Even then, the South
wasn't his cup of tea.

A decade later,
he moved to New York, a jobless
high-school dropout
and sometime Southern Bell hardhat.
Curious, I went to see
his new flat—
at the Des Artistes, no less.

I hadn't spoken to him
in years, and gaped at the slim,
striking young man,
shorter than I,
who'd been drinking Tanqueray
all day, and who began
by saying, "Hi. I'm gay."

He set to work
impressing me, dropping names
by the score: a senator,
a T.V. star, a famed
fashion photographer. It seemed
he'd already befriended or
bedded half New York.

He said: "Oh, what it can *do*
to me, to go to Columbus Avenue
and see that endless parade
of gorgeous men! I don't believe
in love—heaven forbid!—
but I do love
this city, I *do!*"

We drank gin-and-tonics; I spurned
a pass. "You're the most
boring boy in town, *sans doute!*"
"And you're a lousy host."
"Am I?" He winked
coyly, yanked
his jeans off, and passed out.

Years later, Nita in town,
I dined with them
in Brooklyn, where he shared
a loft with a neo-expressionist.
He was, he said,

in love with the artist,
out of love with Manhattan.

He'd stopped drinking,
and told me why:
last May, in his home state,
he'd been booked for DWI,
and used his one phone call
to order a pizza. He'd gone straight
to rehab from jail.

Sober and broke, he hied
back to New York *sans* job or home.
His first day here, a bright
young artist took him
to La Grenouille, and said:
"Move in with me." He did—
that night.

"Darling, I've *always* been
lucky," he bragged to me,
reclining on his sofa like a fat
matron. (He'd put on weight.)
"However long the drop may be,
I always land on my feet."
Nita, sipping gin

beside me, glowed with pride.
Then he left the room

to get a Tab,
and she slipped me a snapshot
of him—so I presumed—
in olive drab.
"His daddy," she confided.

MOUNT HOPE

in memoriam Ruth Hines Thomas

I.

There is no mountain at or near Mount Hope.
It's far from mountains, on the coastal plain,
bounded by airless marshes, dense with sedge,
and acres of farmland, yellow and brown with grain,
just off a two-lane secondary road
at Florence, South Carolina's eastern edge.
The place is quiet, untouched by distress,
and dappled with light; immense and motionless,
the wondrously thriving ancient trees supply
a glorious canopy of branches, leaves,
and sprawling gray-green Spanish moss that weaves
among the boughs, two dozen cubits high,
creating a sanctuary, an abode
where no one (so one feels) will interlope.

II.

The thousand or so people that you knew,
the community of neighbors, kin, and friends
who touched you with their joys, woes, arguments,
are here now, underneath this leaf-strewn ground,

sharing communally their common end.
Each family, as in life, has an address;
here fathers, mothers, brothers, sisters, sons,
daughters, and grandchildren huddle round
a proud name carved upon a monument,
whose sweet and stately sentences express
the love they bore each other. *We all die,*
they say, as if they knew it to be true
each moment of their lives. Beloved one,
the world's a cemetery. Here you lie.

III.

Oh, how the mind, knowing everything, can lie!
Here I stand before our family.
Their names, engraved in stone for eighty years,
have never been much more than names to me—
quaint names in brittle, brown obituaries
which I pencilled into my pedigree
years ago, enthusiastically,
though these nineteenth-century Southern kin
remained less real to me than Pip, Huck Finn,
and Daisy Miller, their contemporaries.
I didn't even know their graves were here,
or think of them, indeed, as having graves,
or lives that led them steadily to the grave,
to marble letters fading year by year.

IV.

But now, between two moments, that has changed.
You're with them now. Time, like a fire curtain,
has come between us, leaving me a store
of sounds and images, vague and disarranged,
pictures that have already begun to fade.
Last night I kept repeating that you can't
be with these dead, you *can't*, it makes no sense;
today I speak of you in the past tense.
Even as I stand in this still glade
on this soft earth, facing the mystery,
my hold upon the past frail and uncertain,
my mind alive with memories that shan't,
in a few years, be with me any more.
I realize that I am history.

V.

Yes, history. For, at your grave, I feel
the earth tug through the damp grass at my heels,
feel my heart insistently pounding, very
deep in my legs and groin and hands and hair,
as if accompanying an old earth song.
I almost think that I can hear that song,
tragic and sweet and natural as breath
or the heaviness of moss-encumbered air;
its grandiose yet simple melody

is, I'm certain, quite unknown to me,
yet strangely familiar, even comforting,
as if, long years ago, I heard you sing
it softly, rocking me gently toward my death.
Dear one, it says, *the world's a cemetery.*

THE JOGGER

"That ye may know": the words, drawn from
    Ephesians
and printed on the Baptist Church marquée,
jar the jogger's dull complacency
and stop him in his tracks on Cherokee.
It's early morning, April; head throbbing, feet
aching, chest tight on this humid street,
throat dry and sore, face damp, brain on fire,
his perspiration soaking through his clothes,
he looks up at the Spartan Baptist spire,
obscenely white in the smogless Southern air,
runs his hand through his disheveled hair,
and thinks of knowledge, and of what he knows.

To the east and west, twin rows
of tall trees hung with Spanish moss
march up the gently curving thoroughfare,
dappling it with shadow.
But here, before the church, there's only sky,
pale blue and infinitely high,
and frightening, somehow; it seems
to testify that knowledge is a dream,
sunrise a deception, the days and years
a device to make an ever-strange life seem
a circuit through familiar ground—

through Sundays, Aprils, hours of sunrise—
instead of what it is: a frighteningly fast
jog out of the Home Place of the past
and into *terra incognita*, a jog past milestones
never seen before, and never to be found
again, on a road that continually solidifies
ahead, and vanishes at the rear...

His eyes fixed on the spire, the jogger
shakes his head. Its whiteness is beyond belief,
the white of perfect light, or bones,
its stately surety a thing of wonder.
Planted in the center of a sprawling lawn,
the church, in the light of dawn,
reminds the jogger of a tomb, and of loss,
of the countless losses that constitute a day,
a life; he imagines a congregation streaming
up the church steps, two hours hence,
like souls on their irrevocable way
through time, and decrement, and immanence.

A distant birdsong stops his dreaming.
Another bird sings back, closer and clearer.
The sun is climbing, squirrels move in the trees,
he feels the morning melting like a fog
and, against his thighs, a pocketful of keys.
The mind, he reflects, could play
its games forever, never coming nearer

to knowledge, inviting only grief.
Thus, wheezing, he looks down from the cross,
straightens out his tight and tangled briefs,
and runs—not slowing to a steady jog
until the steeple is behind him, and he's under
the canopy of trees and Spanish moss,
anticipating today's fried chicken dinner,
wondering if the Braves will win or lose,
hoping exercise will make him thinner.

II

THE VIEW FROM AN AIRPLANE AT NIGHT, OVER CALIFORNIA

This is a sight that Wordsworth never knew,
whether looking down from mountain, bridge, or hill:
An endless field of lights, white, orange, and blue,
as small and bright as stars, and nearly still,
but moving slowly, many miles below,
in blackness, as stars crawl across the skies,
and ranked in rows that stars will never know,
like beads strung on a thousand latticed ties.
Would even Wordsworth, seeing what I see,
know that these lights are not well-ordered stars
that have been here a near-eternity,
but houses, streetlamps, factories, and cars?
Or has this slim craft made too high a leap
above it all, and is the dark too deep?

ON A TRAIN, NEAR MIDNIGHT,
IN THE CALIFORNIA DESERT

Reclining, eyes about to close, I see
blue lights that mark a runway before me.

I turn to the window and espy
the cool, dark Mojave speeding by.

There's a metal clatter, chugging sounds, a door
opens with a *whoosh*; and the porter's flashlight
   swings down the corridor.

PINE CONE

At Kipling and Lytton streets in Palo Alto,
under this small cool tree on this bright blue day,
I almost feel at home. For it almost feels
like a place in my ancestral Southern town—
Coit and Elm, to be particular,
a residential crossroads gone commercial.

On two corners, old frame houses, one a bookstore,
the other a doctor's office; on the third,
a two-story medical complex, rather tiny,
modern and antiseptic, steel and glass.
And here on the fourth, a modest parking lot
where a tall, broad high-school boy in tennis whites
plays with a pine cone, keeping it aloft
from moment to moment with perfect little taps
of his toe, arch, heel, calf, knee, left leg and right.
The minutes pass and yet he never falters,
never fails in poise or energy.
At one point he extends his long left arm
and pops the cone to the tip of his index finger;
the cone rolls down the arm, across his shoulders,
and down the other arm, diving directly
onto a waiting toe, which taps it over
to the heel of his left foot. The little cone
never touches the ground, not for an instant.

After several minutes of this game,
another young man happens on the scene—
bespectacled, slender, smug, and almost girlish
in a fussy red pullover and blue checked shirt.
He prances into the lot and, without a glance
at the tall and broad and dexterous young man,
slides behind the wheel of a red Peugeot;
at which the tall boy, with stunning nonchalance,
drops his pine cone unceremoniously,
swings open the passenger door of the Peugeot,
and throws himself into the bucket seat,
slamming the door behind him. The car drives off,
a long leg jutting boldly from its window,
a large white sneaker signalling a right.

Ten pine cones lie scattered on the asphalt.

ON LEAVING THE ARTISTS' COLONY

The way love rests upon coincidence,
the way a sense of family and home
can flow now, like a stream, through several hearts
transplanted from their diverse native climes
by strangers' choices, violates all sense.

If we had all been here at different times,
I know we'd have formed other loyalties,
drawn other eyes and written other poems,
and I know there are friendships I'd have made
with people whom I now may never meet.

But so be it. Heard melodies are sweet,
and unheard melodies are never played
except on the harmonium of art.
This place we love reminds us how immense
the world is, and how small our cherished part,

and why we feel drawn on toward mysteries,
compelled to paint and sculpt, compose and write.
To think of those who'll be here three months hence,
who'll feel just as we do, and find it hard
believing that emotions so intense

can be so commonplace, is to regard
those mysteries as if with second sight.
It is to sense an elemental rhyme
of soul and soul, to feel a river flow
between our hearts and those we'll never know.

MALIBU, JANUARY

The world is sky, water, and wet sand.
The winter sun burns low in the southwest,
deep orange, elliptical; the sky is streaked
with rose; the waves at the sea's edge are pink.
My white sneakers settle into the sand
beside the Malibu Canal, and start to sink.
A breeze whips at my bare arms and legs,
teasingly, a thing of memory.

Then, down the beach a ways, I notice him:
a solitary boy, graceful, tall, and slim,
stepping from rock to rock along the shore,
heading toward the canal, his white surfboard
and black wetsuit under his arm.
His plaid Bermuda shorts are pastel pink,
his hair blond, nearly white in the sun,
and waving in the sunset wind like wheat.
Reaching the canal a ball's throw from me,
he sets down his board and climbs methodically,
and without haste, into his slick black suit—
first one leg, then the other, then both arms,
as if demonstrating for a class
the proper way to do this sort of thing—
then zips his suit up slowly, sensually,
the sun's bonfire burning at his back.
I watch, beguiled, knowing that when I see

that sun again it will be white as ice,
rising wearily over the cold, gray
New York skyline and wan New Jersey wastes,
as my steel-winged bird descends
and I prepare my overcoat and scarf...

This may not be enough for me, therefore,
this scene, this moment that will slip away
before I can set it firmly in my mind.
But here it is, and it is all there is:
the sky, the sand, the water, and the boy.
He picks his board back up and strolls across
the shallow, narrow, swift, polluted stream
into the Colony. His back to me,
he gleams like a black sea-god in the sun,
heroically, his hair suffused with light,
his board swaying with each step, sporadically
flashing silver as he goes his way.

CALIFORNIA

"My parents are European," he told me,
"but I come from Fresno, a true Californian."
And we went on in the sunless New York afternoon
and our middle European names,
and drank tea, and talked for an hour.

*

Summer '76. I descended
into the grubby pit beneath the Garden—
that Garden where a thousand Democrats
from fifty states, D.C.,
the Virgin Islands, Guam, and the Canal Zone
were, at the moment, busy nominating
a grinning Georgia man for President.
(The winning team!) Downstairs
bag ladies begged change; addicts weaved
or crouched in corners swabbing beads of sweat
with grimy shirt-sleeves from their foreheads.
A humid New York morning.

For three days thereafter we rolled through countryside,
Pennsylvania, Ohio, Indiana,
and the first night out it rained, as if to cleanse us.

Slowly we wound through desert steepnesses,
Colorado, New Mexico, Arizona,
as if ascending to another sphere.

And then we were pacing to and fro
on tiles dark red and brown and indigo,
mysterious gold tiles that clacked under our heels
beneath a hot white sun
at the white brick station, at Barstow.

And in Los Angeles, the City of the Angels,
we smiled at the palm trees and pointed to the houses
which clung, as if by magic, to the sides of hills.
We went to Disneyland, attended the filming
of a commercial for the "test markets,"
and saw Katharine Hepburn at Western Costume.

*

Several summers later I went by air.
Five hours from the East Coast to L.A.,
and half an hour more to the San Joaquin,
where he was waiting under an opal sky.
Handsome, tall, and thoroughly at home
in this land bleached white by a white sun,
he glimpsed me, smiled. We floated to his car
on the hot dry air, turned onto a wide road
between broad, fragrant groves.
"Dates," he nodded, and there they were

in endless, ordered columns. "Figs," he said,
then "walnuts," "apricots."

At home, we parked beneath a spreading palm
and stepped out of the living room's glass doors
into the backyard: orange and lemon trees,
a swimming pool. His Swiss-accented mother
barbecued sirloin steaks. We took a dip.

*

"The valley, please," I tell the cabbie.
"Take Laurel Canyon."

*

My mother came here thirty years ago
and worked for M.G.M., answering fan mail.
The pay was lousy, but she loved the job:
she ran into Van Johnson on the lot
and once sat next to Robert Taylor
in the commissary. She was always
in love with the movies,
always seemed to be watching a movie
at the key moments of her life.
When her water broke, she was roaring
at Marilyn Monroe in *Bus Stop*;
her first date with my father
was Judy Garland in *A Star is Born*;
and the day her father died

in South Carolina, she was in L.A.,
watching Ronald Reagan and Doris Day
in *The Winning Team*. When she got home
the phone was ringing. She packed her things quickly
and left her little flat forever.
They had to put the ramp back
to let her on the plane.

                                    *

In Beverly Hills
the church, the post office, the bank
are identical:
low-lying white structures
on well-tended lawns.
The cabbie, a Mexican, doesn't understand English
and doesn't seem to know his way around.
"Derecha, derecha," I tell him at Sunset.

                                    *

We slept in his old bedroom
under his sister's cheerleading ribbons,
and the next morning drove to San Francisco.
We climbed the cliffs at Golden Gate Park
in the icy morning mist,
shopped at Macy's Union Square,
lunched in Chinatown.
We drove to Davis; he showed me the campus,
a quad with trees. We dined in Sacramento

and I drove back while he slept at my side,
drove through the dark down an unfamiliar freeway,
three hundred miles long and absolutely straight,
drove to Fresno, and was there at two a.m.,
reading the names on signs of deserted streets:
Divisadero, Belmont, Dolores.

*

When my mother left home again,
she did not go west,
but north, to New York. She took an apartment
with two other Southern belles,
a modest secretary and a Copa girl.
One night the Copa girl fixed the secretary up
with a "handsome doctor."
The secretary chickened out, and my mother
went in her place.
The doctor took her to *A Star is Born*
and to half a dozen clubs.
"New York in the fifties," she always sighs to me,
"how things have changed,
how things have changed."

*

"Right here—*aqui*," I tell the taxi driver,
and he pulls over, stops, and lets me out.
Before and behind us, Ventura Boulevard
stretches fifty miles through the long valley,

lined by doughnut places, gallerias,
and roller-skate emporia. Nearby,
the concrete-lined Los Angeles River flows
gently toward the Pacific. Two blocks away
my mother watches T.V. in a dark apartment
with a view of a swimming pool.

*

My mother had always wanted to live in the West.
My father had always wanted to stay in the East.

One night, when I was in high school,
I sat on their bedroom floor,
cataloguing her records from the Forties,
the Andrews Sisters and Frank Sinatra,
when she came in and said,
"He told me it's all right with him
if I move to California."

The next day my father took me
to his old college campus on the Heights.
N.Y.U. was giving way to Bronx Community;
the alumni were giving their last hurrah.

Folding chairs were lined up on the quad,
and ancient men in cap and gown
sang songs *"of Lydia Pinkham
and her love for the human race*

how she sells her vegetable compound
and the papers publish her face"
and held a ceremony on the quad,
on the grass under the spreading trees,
that I did not understand.

My father and I walked through the Hall of Fame,
he recalling his undergraduate days,
I inspecting the statuary.
Luther Burbank had been spray-painted red,
Ben Franklin's left ear was clubbed out of shape,
and Thomas Jefferson lay at the bottom of a hill.
"It's all coming to an end, all of it,"
my father said. And we walked on, slowly,
and found our way to the Library,
which was empty and untended,
and wandered among the shelves,
and walked off with a copy of *Pravda*.

III

GRAND CENTRAL STATION, 20 DECEMBER 1987

in memoriam M. J. G.

The clock's so huge you can watch the minute hand
crawl steadily toward three. It's after one
on a gray and drizzly Sunday afternoon
before Christmas, and all around me stand

handsome young men who look like paradigms
of American youth. Poised, affluent, and clean-
cut in sweaters that read *Princeton* and *Penn,*
they chat idly, glancing from time to time

at their luggage, and at the clock; they're on
their way to Westport, Mahopac, and Rye,
to houses set beneath a still blue sky,
each with its Porsche, its wide and quiet lawn,

its complement of trees—elm, maple, birch—
and to an exurban sense of harmony
synonymous, for them, with home. And me?
I'm going to a Hastings-on-Hudson church

to say farewell to one who should have been,
sixteen years hence, a freshman Ivy Leaguer
heading home for Christmas—bright, slim, eager
to see his parents, waiting for a train.

AUGUST

August already past its midpoint,
the falling action, the impotent
feeling of motion toward a closure,
summer starts to take its shape
in dreams, where, rambling down some
amalgam of the Boulevard Carnot
and Mommsenstrasse, through crowds
of Teutonic blonds and olive-skinned
Mediterraneans, every now and then
stepping into a shop, or stopping
for a bite at a sidewalk café, I swap
elementary utterances with locals,
now a *nochmal*, now a *je voudrais*,
and now a *goodbye*, the languages
merged, the world a single street.

SIXTY-FIFTH STREET POEMS
for Christopher

1. BEGINNING

Love, here we stand at the beginning
of our life together, and I find myself
thinking of a hot summer night
in my seventeenth year, when I lay
alone in a strange room, in a dormitory bed
for the first time in my life, too scared
to rise, too thrilled to sleep. The dark
screamed out "The Night Chicago Died,"
and indeed it was as if something had died
and something were being born. In other rooms,
I knew, the boys and girls I'd met that day
were doing things that were a mystery
to me; I felt apart from them—and yet,
that night, a part of all they were.
For though I recognized I'd never really
be one of them, and wasn't yet aware
I wasn't quite the boy my parents knew,
it was as if that night I realized,
somewhere deep within, that I'd discover
myself in much the way a geometry student
swings a compass from one place, then another,
to find a unique point.

2. GLOVES

It's barely the middle of January,
and already the black leather gloves
you bought me for Christmas are ruined,
stiff and water-lined, their proud shine gone.
They spent night before last in the gutter,
in melting snow, and it wasn't till morning
that I missed them, and ran outside
to find them soaked. However did it happen?
All day I'd been so careful, keeping them
in my coat pocket, neatly folded,
constantly reaching in and touching them
to make sure they were there. All I
could think of was the price tag I'd glimpsed
by accident: a hundred dollars.
So precious, and so losable! They seemed
almost as much a burden as a gift, but when
I tried to give them back you shook your head.
"I want you to have the best," you said.
I kept them. And since I couldn't bring myself
either to show them off or hide them away
in a bedroom drawer, I carried them
around in my pocket, invisible to the world,
every so often stroking them gingerly
with my fingertips. Until the other night
when, unwittingly, I let them fall,
in silent darkness, into the gray, wet snow.

3. AUGUST NIGHT

A quarter after midnight, and the light
from Sloan Kettering, soft and yellow,
touches your face upon the pillow,
here in our darkened room. My right
hand meanders through your hair, straight
and freshly cut; my left hand follows
your breath, in and out. I whisper: "Hello."
"Hello," you breathe. Smooth and white,
your face glows softly, like the moon,
and I stare at you silently, stunned
by the testimony of my eyes.
A year ago, this might have been the moon.
Now it's home. Day by day I wonder
at the glory of these nights and days.

4. BEDTIME

Turning out the light, I take
three steps to our bed, climb in,
and pull the covers over me,
making certain you're covered too.
In the dark, I lie facing you,
nearly touching, hearing you breathe.
Gently I reach out, stroke
your back, and you sigh softly,

happily, still asleep. Can this
be my life? It's almost been
a year, yet this bed, these bare
walls, still seem sheer bliss,
undeserved by me, a cosmic blunder
let pass for another blessed day.
Like an émigré breathing free air,
I fret even as I weep with wonder.

5. BOOKSHELVES

On the industrial fringe of Park Slope
one hot summer morning, we carried the boards
that would be our bookshelves onto President Street,
and tied the long pieces, with a hundred feet
of rope, onto the roof of my old car.
Our new home in Manhattan seemed so far,
I feared the knots would unravel, the cords
snap in two, the wood break free of the rope.
It didn't. We made it home, and built the shelves.
And when friends visited, they made a fuss:
could shelves so fine be made by such as we?
"Did you *really* build them?" they kept asking us.
We did...and much besides. And nobody
has marveled at it all more than ourselves.

6. CONFIRMATION

for Christopher, born a Seventh-day
Adventist and confirmed in the
Episcopal Church, 5 November 1989

How is it that an old devotion calls
across the years, and in a different key,
discovering you in this far, foreign place,
heart harnessed to and bedstead shared with me?
How to discern the turnings of a grace
that waits long years to raise a soul that falls
out of its palm—and, in another land
finding it, lifts with a different hand?

7. THE GARDEN OF EARTHLY DELIGHTS

It was a June morning, and we'd met
the night before, and walking you
to the subway in the warm, bright
day, down streets numbingly familiar
to me, and entirely strange to you,
wanting desperately to ask if we might
see each other again, but afraid
that in my callowness I'd be over-
stepping a boundary, I was overjoyed
when you posed the question yourself:
and so, that Saturday night, we met
in the Village for a proper date,
a hamburger at McBell's and a play,

which I now recall as a fantasy
of lights and a rhapsodic whirling
of bodies in midair: "The Garden
of Earthly Delights."

8. Remembering the Artists' Colony

I'd come from New York, an alien in that land,
and for six weeks the congregations of cattle
on the sun-drenched slopes of the naked yellow hills,
the spotted deer at the far end of the meadow
behind the house, before the wall of pine,
the gray-white sheep under the olive trees,
and the stony creek at the heart of the dark ravine
under a high church ceiling of pine and redwood
whispered insistently: *you must change your life.*
Or whispered, rather, that I could, I *could*,
that even such as I might find love in this world,
might find another life, and find it good.

LENOX HILL

"Virtue is to the soul what health is to the body."
—*La Rochefoucauld*

A month from ninety, my grandmother lay
drawn and dappled under immaculate sheets,
intubated from stem to stern. Each day
at lunchtime, that March, I came
to watch her down a purée
of carrots and spinach and meat,
to listen to her mumble "home...home,"
and to hover in the doorway, leaning on the frame.

Each day, if I lingered long enough, he'd pass
eventually: a young man, about
my age, in a cotton robe
and slippers, his delicate
fingers clutching an I.V. stand.
Each time he passed,
our eyes met and he smiled;
and I smiled back, feeling he'd bared
his soul, and I'd seen it was good.
One day, he had company: a careworn
older woman, and a tall friend
beside whom he looked frail,
but whose handsome features flared
with terror, while his radiated
serenity. Even then, passing me, he smiled.

My grandmother recovered
and was released. On her last day there,
while we awaited a nurse who'd gone
in search of a chair, I went down the hall
and noted the name by his door.
A month later, it turned up in tiny, austere
print on the narrow-columned page
that had become, a year
or so earlier, my daily reading. In separate
notices, four friends and his lover
described the young man as I'd known
him through his smile: as sweet, unscared,
affectionate. But the notice I read again
and again was the third,
which called him "a beautiful
and unusual person" who "never failed
to express gratitude to those who cared
for and loved him," and declared
simply: "I will never forget him." The signer
identified herself as the young man's
"substitute mother"; her surname,
I noticed, was the same as that of his lover.

POEMS FOR CHIP

1. A SUNDAY VISIT

Your new and solitary room in Riverdale
was high-ceilinged, white-walled, Spartan:
a small bookcase, a modest Fragonard,
a tiny wooden cross centered on a Bible.
The black spinet was altar-like, austere.
In an otherwise naked corner, a Bach *Konzert*
sat on a stand. The cot I recognized.
You made us tea, and as the sky shaded
from gray to black, we spoke with quiet urgency
of art and faith, of love and its frustrations.
Grasping in slender fingers a slender slice
of apple, you looked into my eyes, then his,
your blue eyes luminous, and confessed,
with a reserved boy's gentle unreserve,
the abiding hunger of your flesh and spirit.
You said that you were "desperately lonely,"
and told us—softly, simply—that we were lucky
to have found each other. The rest was left
unspoken: how lucky we were to be together
in this white room, to have this intimate
afternoon and evening of tea and apple,
how lucky to have the opportunity
to examine these three filaments, our souls,
and to find them even more homologous
and intricately interwoven than we'd imagined.

2. FERRY

On the day of the solemnity
of the conversion of St. Paul,
surrounded by evening and by the small
lights that ring the Upper Bay,

we stand silently at the ferry's bow,
possessed by the engine's basso thrum
(like the steady pulsing of some
mighty heart), and stare with awe

at the metropolitan towers, stark
and radiant and immense
as an ultramundane dream of reverence,
rising into January's dark

night, dead ahead across the bay,
and approaching us, do what we
may, as slowly and implacably
as the future, as death, as Judgment Day.

Another hour, and we'll surrender today
to memory: this day that began
with an extemporaneous sermon
by the bishop, for his own name-day,

on another Paul, on grace and the void,
and on the epistolary text: "he which
persecuted us in times past now preacheth
the faith which once he destroyed."

St. Paul, the bishop said, had been
a sexist, "with social views I can't condone.
And yet..." And yet somehow he'd known
exactly what it means to be a Christian.

The bishop recalled his own
road to Damascus: year after year,
he'd denied his vocation. Came the war,
and he nursed battle-blasted men,

their bodies repulsive, shattered.
Only afterwards did he realize
that when he'd stared into their eyes
he'd seen the eyes of the Lord.

For, he told us, that's where God
resides: in the flesh,
in the corrupt, imperfect flesh,
"in the flesh of everybody

around you—your closest friend,
the homeless man on the curb,

your lover." Yes, that was the word
he used: *lover*. And when I turned

to you, your blue eyes were burning red,
your face wet with tears,
as if all your twenty-three years
had been comprehended in what he said.

ART AND WORSHIP

"But Bruce, why can't you worship art?"
—*H. Z.*

However it may help us to transcend
or comprehend this vast, impermanent
realm where we commingle and contend,
furnishing us, as it were, with wings,
art is a means of worship, not an end,
the way we formulate, share, and present
to the far-off and unfathomed firmament
the yearnings of our souls toward higher things.

If a sculpture, story, symphony,
or some stray strain played on a violin
seems to articulate a verity
resoundingly, it is because it springs
out of a kindred sensibility,
soaring above the universal din
to remind us all that we are kin
with anyone whom song inspires to sing.

And yet there is an all-surpassing thrill
toward which the highest art can only tend,
as circumstance, facility, and will,
and all divine endowment will allow;
the more immaculately to distill,
with every small degree it may ascend,

that which is eternally beyond,
and which we humbly ponder and avow.

To glorify a man, or venerate
his works, is therefore racial vanity;
revering art, we falsely elevate
ourselves, and fail to see that, here below
the height, our art is to articulate
that which we witness only partially,
finding forms for what we know must be,
yet can't be understood by what we know.

DEVOTIONS

For the longest time, he dismissed it
as a vestige of childhood—that evening prayer
he'd faithfully recited, night after night,
alone in bed, until his twenty-third year.

He'd stopped abruptly. A strange affair:
one friendly embrace, and the haze
obscuring his heart had scattered, disclosing
the abominable hunger harbored there.

He sought godless virtue. He let his heart
lead him to water, yet never drank.
Year after year, he frequented the rank
barrooms, staring, thirsting, standing apart.

His only lovers he conjured in solitude.
Miraculously beautiful and wise,
they were virtuous, as one of flesh and blood
couldn't be. It shone in their eyes.

Years passed. Then, on a spring night
no different from any other, a benign face
appeared before him, and two radiant eyes.
Falling in love, he fell...or so he thought,

till one day in almost-winter it struck
like thunder in his breast: not only his flesh
was taking long-sought nourishment from flesh.
Quietly, too, his soul had been partaking.

Flesh had come accompanied by grace; the light
in his love's eyes was the love of God.
It was that which filled him, night after night,
in his love's warm arms. And so he prayed.

Bruce Bawer is author of *Diminishing Fictions* (Graywolf Press), a collection of criticism about the modern American novel. He is a regular contributor to *The New Criterion*, and has written for *The American Scholar*, *Commentary*, *The Nation*, and *Connoisseur*. His poems have appeared in *Boulevard*, *The Hudson Review*, and *Poetry*. His collection *Prophets and Professors: Essays on the Lives and Works of Modern Poets*, is forthcoming from Story Line Press.

Book design by Lysa McDowell

This book was set in Palatino type
using Aldus PageMaker on a Macintosh computer.

Book printing by Edwards Brothers